The Usborne
Bedtime Treasury

The Usborne
Bedtime Treasury

Rosie Dickins

Illustrated by Raffaella Ligi

Edited by Jenny Tyler and Lesley Sims

Designed by Nicola Butler,
Laura Fearn and Jessica Johnson

Contents

The
Bedtime Fairy

As the sun sank over Fairyland, the Bedtime
Fairy reached for her storybook. Each night,
when the small fairies were tucked up in bed,
she read them a bedtime story.

"What shall it be tonight?" she wondered.
"An old tale or something new?"

She opened the book, and magic crackled in the air.
Dragons and mermaids peeked out of the pages, and a genie
popped up in clouds of smoke. In one story, elves and goblins
were playing tag by moonlight. In another, a white bear padded
through drifts of sparkling snow.

"Brrrr," shivered the Bedtime Fairy, as snowflakes blew
out of the story and into the room. She turned the page, to reveal
a crowd of dancing mice... Then she yawned.

"All these stories are making me sleepy," she sighed.
"I need a nap." She shut the book and closed her eyes.
A minute later, she was fast asleep.

7

A breeze stirred the curtains,
fluttering the pages of the book.
Curious faces peered out. Then a goblin
jumped boldly out of his page
and into the room.

"Sssh, she's asleep," he whispered.
"Let's explore!"

He tiptoed away. One by one, the other story creatures
followed, creeping down the hall and into the kitchen.

"What shall we do now?" asked a dragon.

"Let's make a cake," suggested a greedy elf.

"Ooh yes," cried the other elves, pulling out a bowl.
Everyone began hunting for ingredients.

"Flour, eggs, sugar..." listed the first elf, stirring them
together with a magic wand. "What else goes in cake?"

"Raisins," said the genie, pouring in a potful.

"What about this?" called the goblin, waving another
little pot in the air. "Atishoo! Oh no, that's pepper."

"Cheese," squeaked the mice. "Let's make cheese cake!"

So the elf added some slices of hard yellow cheese.
He prodded the mix doubtfully with the wand.

"This doesn't look much like cake."

"It needs cooking," said the dragon. "Allow me."

He breathed hot flames over the bowl.
A smell of burned cheese filled the air.
"Watch out, it's catching fire!" cried the white bear.
The elf backed away, dropping the wand –
which clattered to the floor, shooting out spells...
Suddenly, the kitchen chairs came to life and chased each
other around the table. Pots and pans banged and clanged,
and the cake exploded in a shower of crumbs.

9

The racket woke the Bedtime Fairy. She jumped up and saw the book lying open - empty - beside her.

"Oh no," she exclaimed. "What's happening?"

She ran to the kitchen. "What a mess," she cried, grabbing her wand. "Abracadabra, cadabra, cazoom!" There was a flash of light and a puff of smoke... and when the smoke cleared, everything was back to normal.

The story creatures sighed with relief.

"You saved us," they told the Bedtime Fairy gratefully.

"But not our cake," added a small, sad elf.

"Look again," said the Bedtime Fairy, smiling.

The elf looked - and cheered. There, on the table, was a perfect cake, deliciously squashy, with cherries on the top.

After everyone had had a slice, the Bedtime Fairy went and got the storybook. One by one, the creatures dived back inside, curling up comfortably between the covers.

Then the clock on the wall chimed.

"Five minutes to bedtime," cried the Bedtime Fairy. "I must hurry!" She reached the small fairies just in time.

"Are you ready for your bedtime story?" she asked them, sitting down at the end of their bed.

"Oh yes," they chorused happily.

So the Bedtime Fairy opened her book once again, and began to read...

The Elves
and the Shoemaker

There was once a poor shoemaker who was so poor,
he couldn't even afford to buy any more leather. He was
down to his last few scraps...

"Just enough for a small pair of slippers," he decided.
So he set to work cutting out the pieces. But when it came
to stitching them together, his eyelids began to droop.

"Time for bed," said his wife, coming in with a candle.
"You can finish those tomorrow."

The next morning, he stumbled sleepily downstairs –
and gasped in amazement. There, instead of the leather,
was a pretty pair of slippers, neatly stitched, with satin bows.
"Who on earth did that?" he wondered.

He sold the slippers for a gold coin, and bought
enough leather to make two pairs of boots.
But again, he found his eyes closing
as he threaded his needle...

11

"I'll finish these tomorrow," he yawned.

But by morning, instead of the leather, there were two pairs of gleaming boots, neatly stitched, with shiny brass buckles.

And so it went on. Each day, the shoemaker bought and cut his leather, and each night, someone else stitched it into the most beautiful boots and shoes.

Soon, business was booming – but the shoemaker and his wife had no idea who was helping them.

So one night, instead of going to bed, they hid behind a curtain and watched...

About midnight, two tiny creatures came in, dressed only in rags. They seized the leather and began stitching. Their tiny fingers flew cleverly until they had finished a whole row of shiny new shoes. And then they left.

"Elves!" exclaimed the shoemaker at last.

"Poor little things," said his wife. "Wearing nothing but rags! Let's make them some proper clothes, to thank them for their help."

The shoemaker nodded.

That day, instead of cutting out human shoes, he made two tiny elf-sized pairs of boots, and his wife sewed two tiny elf-sized suits. At bedtime, they laid everything on the workbench and hid again.

About midnight, the elves came in – and skipped for joy to find such fine new clothes. They put them on at once and danced out of the door, singing...

We look so smart in our new suits,
Too smart by far
for stitching boots!

The shoemaker and his wife watched, smiling. They didn't mind losing their magic helpers. Now, they had plenty of money and plans for new shoes...

They were back in business, thanks to the elves.

13

Clever Kallie

Two brothers, Karl and Kaspar, both kept their horses in the same field. Karl had a patient brown mare, and Kaspar a magnificent chestnut stallion.

One day, they were bringing in the horses with Karl's daughter, Kallie, when they saw a little brown foal standing beside the stallion.

"It's mine," said Kaspar at once. "Look, my stallion has had a foal."

"Don't be ridiculous," replied Karl. "Stallions don't have foals! It must be my mare's – which makes it mine."

"But it's closer to my stallion," insisted Kaspar.

The brothers argued and argued – until eventually the local prince heard about their dispute. He decided to settle matters by asking three riddles. "Whoever gives the best answers will win the foal," he announced.

Kaspar grinned. "I'm so clever," he thought happily. "I'm bound to win."

But Karl's face fell. "What will I do?" he muttered. "I'm no good at riddles."

"Don't worry," Kallie told him. "I'll help you."

"First," said the prince, "what is the fastest thing in the world?"

"Easy," said Kaspar proudly. "My stallion!"

Standing on tiptoe, Kallie whispered in Karl's ear, and he repeated what she said. "But no horse can outrun the wind. The wind is faster."

The prince nodded thoughtfully. "Next, what is the heaviest thing in the world?"

"Iron," said Kaspar at once. "Just try carrying some!"

Again, Kallie whispered and Karl repeated, "But the ground is heavier. It's so heavy, no one can pick it up!"

The prince laughed. "Lastly, what is the most important thing in the world?"

Kaspar snorted. "Money, of course," he answered.

Kallie shook her curls. She whispered, and Karl repeated, "Money can buy many things, but it can't buy an honest man. I say honesty is more important."

The words made Kaspar blush - for of course he knew the foal really belonged to his brother.

The prince smiled. "The foal is yours," he told Karl. "Thanks to your daughter. Take good care of them both. I only wish all my advisors were as clever as Kallie!"

Tom Thumb

There was once a farmer's wife who longed for a son.

"Even if he was no bigger than my thumb," she sighed.

The very next day, she found a red tulip under her window. It had sprung up overnight.

"How did that happen?" she wondered, gazing at the flower. "Oh!" There, inside the scarlet petals, was a tiny boy – no bigger than a thumb. "A fairy must have heard my wish," she said happily.

Softly, she called her husband. "Look," she whispered.

"Let's name him Tom."

The couple were delighted with their tiny son, although his size often got him into trouble.

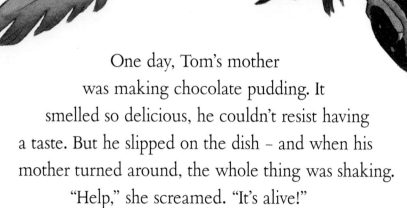

One day, Tom's mother
was making chocolate pudding. It
smelled so delicious, he couldn't resist having
a taste. But he slipped on the dish – and when his
mother turned around, the whole thing was shaking.

"Help," she screamed. "It's alive!"

"No, ma, it's me," cried Tom, waving a chocolatey
arm. "I don't think I like pudding so much any more."

His mother scooped him up and gave him a bath in a
teacup. "Why don't you pick some strawberries for dinner,"
she suggested, when he was dry again.

So Tom went outside. He had just picked a big, juicy
berry when a hungry bird flew up. A moment later,
Tom and his berry were high in the air.

"Let go!" he shouted. Startled, the bird did so, and Tom
tumbled down – splash! He plunged into a rushing river,
where enormous fish were swimming. One of the fish
opened its mouth, and everything went dark.

That night, the King was giving a grand banquet.
The first course was an enormous fish – and, when it was
cut open, out jumped Tom.

"Goodness me," exclaimed the King. "Who are you?"

17

"And what are you doing in my dinner?"

So Tom explained, "...and the fish was caught by a fisherman, and here I am," he finished.

The King smiled. "You're very brave," he told Tom. "You should be a knight." And he gave Tom a needle for a sword, and a tame mouse for a horse. "From now on, you will be known as Sir Tom."

The guests applauded, and the banquet was continuing, when suddenly a maid shrieked. "A rat!" Around the hall, people climbed onto chairs to get away from it.

Tom seized his needle and leaped onto his mouse.

The rat had little yellow eyes and long, sharp teeth, but Tom wasn't afraid.

"Charge!" he yelled.

He galloped straight at it, waving the needle.

The rat squealed and fled.

Everyone cheered. "Hurrah for Sir Tom!"

But Tom knew he couldn't be a knight forever.

"My parents will be worried," he said. "I must go home."

The King nodded. "I will give you a parting gift," he said. He showed Tom a chest full of treasure. "Take whatever you can carry!"

Tom stared in wonder. Gold shone and jewels glittered... but they were all much too heavy. Then, among the heaps of coins, he spotted a little silver penny.

"I'll have that," he said. "Thank you!"

It was very late by the time Tom rode up to the familiar farmhouse. His parents were thrilled to have him safely back.

"Where have you been?" they cried, when they had finished hugging him.

"On an adventure," replied Tom. "I met the King and made my fortune." He proudly pulled out his silver penny.

"But it's good to be home again," he added, stifling a yawn. "It's been a busy day, and now I think it's time for bed."

The Fisherman
and the Genie

There was once a young fisherman who lived by a lake.
Each morning, he went down to the shore and cast his net.
And each evening, he came home with a basket full
of fine, fat fish.

But one morning, when he drew in his net, he found only a few
stones and shells and an old glass bottle, its sides misty with age.

"This weighs a ton," he muttered, pulling it out of the net.

"I wonder what's inside?"

He shook it, but there was no sound. He pulled out the cork
and sniffed, but there was no smell. He tipped it up, but nothing
came out. "Empty," he decided, dropping it on the sand.

Suddenly, smoke began pouring out. The fisherman stepped
back in alarm. The smoke grew bigger and bigger,
bubbling and boiling...

"A genie!" cried the fisherman in astonishment, as a fierce face formed out of the smoke.

"Yes," boomed the genie. "Ah, it's good to be free. Now for something to eat... I think I'll start with you!"

"Please don't!" begged the fisherman, as huge hands stretched towards him. "After all, I let you out – don't I deserve your thanks?"

"I don't care," growled the genie. "I'm too hungry after being cooped up in that bottle for so long."

The fisherman thought fast. "Surely a great genie like you wasn't trapped in that itty-bitty bottle," he said.

"Do you doubt what I say?" thundered the genie.

"Well, I don't understand how you got inside," continued the fisherman. "You're so big and powerful...
I really can't believe it without seeing it!"

"Then watch this, fool," snapped the genie, whooshing back into the bottle.

As soon as the last wisp of smoke disappeared, the fisherman rammed in the cork.

"And there you'll stay," he told the bottle,
"until you learn to say thank you!"

Starlight Wishes

Each night, at bedtime, Stella looked up at
the sky and whispered:

"Star light, star bright,
First star I see tonight,
Wish I may, wish I might,
Have the wish I wish tonight."

And each night, her wish was the same – to visit the stars
in the sky. "They're so beautiful," she sighed.

But the nights passed and her wish didn't come true.
So, one day, Stella set off to find the stars herself.

She walked and walked, until she came to a stream.
"Good morning," said Stella. "I'm looking for the
stars in the sky, have you seen them?"

"Oh yes," gushed the stream. "They shine on my
banks at night. Splash around and you might find one."

Stella took off her shoes and waded into the water,
but all she found were pebbles. So she got out,
dried her feet and went on.

She walked and walked, until she came to a pond.
"Good afternoon," said Stella. "I'm looking for
the stars in the sky, have you seen them?"

"Oh yes," gurgled the pond. "They shine in my face at night. Fish around and you might find one." So Stella picked up a long branch and fished.

But all she caught was an old boot.

Now Stella was very tired and it was getting dark. She walked until she came to a meadow full of tiny, dancing creatures. They were so pretty and bright, for a moment she thought she had found the stars. But then she saw their wings and realized they were fairies.

"Good evening," said Stella. "I'm looking for the stars in the sky, have you seen them?"

"Why yes," cried the fairies. "They shine on the grass here at night. Dance with us and you may meet one."

So Stella danced with the fairies, and her tiredness fell away.

She danced and danced, but no stars came.

And then she sat down and cried.

"Oh no, don't cry," said the fairies kindly.
"If you really want to reach the stars, we'll tell
you the way. Ask Four Feet to take you to No Feet,
and ask No Feet to take you to the Stepless Stair..."

So Stella walked on. Before long, she met a white horse
with silver hooves.

"Are you Four Feet?" asked Stella. "I'm looking for the stars
in the sky. Can you take me to No Feet?"

"Yes," neighed the horse. "Climb up."

They galloped over the land until they came to the sea.
Far off, a rainbow arched into the sky. Stella looked around –
and spotted a fish with a silver tail.

"No Feet," said Stella. "I'm looking for the stars in the sky.
Can you take me to the Stepless Stair?"

"Yes," gurgled the fish. "Jump on."

They swam over the sea, until they reached the rainbow.
"The Stepless Stair," thought Stella – and she began to climb.

As she went higher, the air grew colder. At the top,
the rainbow glittered with frost. Stella looked around
in delight. The brightest stars sparkled like diamonds.
The smallest stars glowed like pearls.

"Welcome, child," called the stars, their voices
chiming like bells. "How did you find us?"

So Stella told them.

Suddenly, with shouts
of excitement, some of
the stars began to fall.
"Quick, make a wish,"
cried one as it zoomed past.
"Wish upon a falling star!"
Now, tired but happy, Stella knew
exactly what she wanted. "I wish I was
home in my nice, warm bed."
No sooner were the words out of her mouth
than she found herself sliding down the rainbow.
She slid faster and faster, until everything was a blur –
and then landed somewhere soft and snug and familiar.
She was back in bed. Smiling, she curled up under the covers
and fell asleep – to dream all night about the stars.

The Miller's Boy
and the Mermaid

There was once a poor miller's boy who lived by a river. One day, he was out cutting reeds when he stumbled and... splash! His knife disappeared into the deep, dark water. "How will I get it back?" he wondered.

"I'll help," came a musical voice. The boy looked up – and gasped. A mermaid with long, flowing hair had appeared in the river. She dived down and returned holding a knife made of solid gold.

The boy looked at it longingly, but he knew it wasn't his. "I'm afraid that's the wrong one," he admitted.

The mermaid dived again, returning with a knife of shining silver. The boy admired it very much, but...

"That's not mine either," he sighed.

So the mermaid dived once more, returning with a rusty old iron knife. "That's it!" cried the boy. "Thank you."

"Such honesty deserves a reward," said the mermaid with a smile. And she laid all three knives – iron, silver and gold – on the bank, before disappearing back under the water with a flick of her tail.

The old miller's eyes lit up when he saw the knives and heard how his son came by them. "That's an easy way to make a living," he thought. "I wonder..."

He picked up the iron knife and hurried out to the river.

Splash! The knife disappeared into the water.

"How will I get it back?" he exclaimed loudly.

"I'll help," said the mermaid, appearing as before. She dived down and returned with a gleaming golden knife.

"Thank goodness you found it," said the miller, reaching out eagerly.

The mermaid frowned. "There's no goodness in lying," she snapped. "This isn't yours, and you know it!" And she vanished, leaving the miller empty-handed.

"I should have known better," he told his son sadly. "It just goes to show, it's always best to be honest."

The Sandman

It was long past bedtime, but Hal couldn't get to sleep. He was snuggled comfortably under the covers and the light was out, but he was still wide awake. So when a little old man came tiptoeing into his room, he sat up at once.

"Who are you?" he asked curiously.

The man jumped and dropped something – and a cloud of glittering golden dust spilled across the floor.

"Oh dear!" he cried. He turned to Hal. "My name is Old Luke," he said. "But most people call me the Sandman."

"The Sandman!" gasped Hal. "I've heard of you, but I didn't know you were real. Mother says you scatter sleepydust, to fill people's dreams with stories, and that's why I find it in my eyes in the morning."

"Yes," said Luke. "I had some wonderful
stories for you, but now they're spilled...
oh dear, oh dear... what shall I do?"

Hal thought for a moment. "Can't you make up some
new stories?" he suggested.

Luke nodded – then snapped his fingers. "I can do better
than that," he said. "I can show you!"

Luke pointed his umbrella at the flowerpot on the
windowsill. Immediately, the flower sprouted long
shoots, which thickened into branches, until it seemed
as if Hal's bed was under a tree laden
with sweet-smelling blossoms.

At the same time, there was a noise from the desk.
It was Hal's homework. He had been copying out his
alphabet, but his writing wasn't very good yet, and the
letters were slipping and sliding all over the place.

"We can't stand up straight," they grumbled.

"You wrote us wonky."

"Then you must be rubbed out," said Luke sternly.

"No, no!" cried the letters, and they all stood up very neatly.

Luke pointed his umbrella at the picture on the wall.
It showed a silver sailing ship on a shining blue sea - only now
the sails were billowing in the wind and the deck was bobbing
up and down. Luke lifted Hal up through the picture frame,
into the sunlight.

The ship sailed past green islands, where toy soldiers
guarded fairytale castles. Princesses waved to Hal from the
castle windows, and the soldiers saluted smartly.

A flock of seabirds flew chattering overhead. To his surprise,
Hal found he could understand them.

"Follow us," they sang, "and see the world! Discover desert
islands where pirates hide their treasure in the sand,
meet monkeys in the shade of the jungle or watch dolphins
playing in the ocean..."

"Oh yes," cried Hal. But before he could hear more,
Luke snapped his fingers and they were back in Hal's room.

"We mustn't be late
for the wedding," Luke told him.

"What wedding?" asked Hal.

"The mouse wedding, of course," replied Luke.

Luke tapped his umbrella, and Hal found himself
shrinking down to the size of a mouse and creeping through
a hole in the skirting board.

On the other side was a hall hung with shimmering cobwebs.
Families of mice were dancing merrily, and beckoned Hal to join
in. But when it came to the wedding feast, Luke said they had to
go. "Ugh!" he muttered. "I can't stand mouse food – all cheese
crumbs and bacon rinds."

As they crept back into Hal's room, the clock in the hall
struck a quarter to midnight.

"What time is it?" asked Luke.

"Why, nearly tomorrow," yawned Hal, climbing into bed.

"Then I must rush," said Luke. "By morning, I must make sure
the stars have gone to bed and the sun is ready to shine..."
And, with a twirl of his umbrella, he was gone.

But Hal didn't see him go. He was already asleep, and dreaming
of sailing in a silver ship, to islands piled high with pirate gold.

Fairy Moon

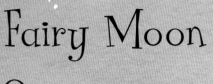

Once upon a time, in Fairyland, the nights were never completely dark. Instead, they were lit by a special shining lantern, which the fairies called the Moon. The Moon hung at the top of Fairyland's tallest tree, and every day a Moon-keeper climbed up to polish it, so its light would never fade.

But one day, after the Moon-keeper left, the branch holding the Moon snapped. The Moon rolled away, unseen, and disappeared down a deep, dark hole.

That night, when the sun set, the sky turned an inky black. Unable to see, fairies tripped over toadstools and elves bumped into dwarfs.

Below ground, things were even worse...

The Moon had fallen into a cave full of trolls. They liked living in the dark, so the sudden moonlight dazzled them. They began blundering around and bumping into things, making an awful din.

The fairies flew to find the Moon-keeper.

"Please do something," they begged. "We need the Moon!"

"I'll find it," he promised. "It can't have gone far."
And, borrowing a candle, he set off bravely into the dark.

He searched and searched, behind shadowy bushes and branches, but the Moon was nowhere to be seen.

"What shall I do?" he groaned.

With a whirring of wings, an owl landed beside him.

"Don't give up," it hooted wisely. "If you can't find the Moon above ground, you must look below."

So the Moon-keeper searched and searched, through echoing caves and caverns, until at last he saw a familiar shining shape... "There it is," he sighed.

"Is this thing yours?" bellowed the trolls.

"Take it away, please! It hurts our eyes."

As soon as the Moon-keeper reached the
surface, a huge cheer went up. "The Moon is back!"
"The Moon-Keeper has rescued the Moon!" Elves and dwarfs
danced for joy, while fairies fluttered up to thank him.

But the Moon-keeper was still worried. "I suppose the
Moon should go back in the tree," he said. "But what if
a branch snaps again?"

"I have a better idea," hooted the owl. "Climb onto my
back and hold tight." Then it spread its wings and soared
into the night. The Moon-keeper gasped as Fairyland spread
out beneath them.

Together, they hung the Moon from the dome of the sky.
Once again, a peaceful silver light covered the land, while
the troll caves were quiet and dark. And, all across Fairyland,
fairies, elves and dwarfs yawned, stretched
and settled down to sleep.

Ice Dragon

One cold winter night, George and Jane were in
their garden watching a bonfire blaze scarlet and gold.
In the distance, they could see more fires – but those fires
glowed mysteriously pink and green and blue.

"They're so beautiful," sighed Jane, gazing dreamily into
the distance. "What are they?"

"The Northern Lights, I think," answered George.
He watched the distant flames bobbing and beckoning...

"Let's go and find out," said Jane.

George nodded, and they set off. As they walked, it grew
very cold. Soon, they were crunching over snow. Then they
started to notice the animals – white rabbits and foxes...

"And that's a polar bear, I'm sure," said Jane.

A little later, they came to a road unlike any they had
ever seen. It was paved with ice and lined with frosty trees.
Moonbeams and stars were strung along the trees to light
the way, and a sign made of silvery snow spelled out:

"This way to the North Pole."

"Come on," cried George. They went slipping and sliding
down the road, until suddenly, they heard a shout.

"Hey, you there. Stop!" It was a hunter with a gun, standing
by a trembling goose. "Do you have any bullets?" he asked.

"No," said George. "Just a slingshot. Why?"

"I want to shoot this snow goose," replied the hunter.

"Oh no," cried George and Jane together. "We won't help
you do that!" And the goose was very grateful.

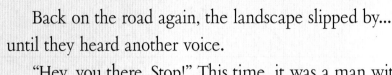

Back on the road again, the landscape slipped by...
until they heard another voice.

"Hey, you there. Stop!" This time, it was a man with
a butterfly net. "Can you lend me a needle?" he asked.

"No," said Jane. "But I can lend you a pin." She began
unfastening the brooch on her coat. "What's it for?"

"To pin this Arctic moth," answered the man,
pointing to his net. George and Jane looked at
each other. Then, while George explained that they
wouldn't help him do that, Jane quietly opened the
net and let the moth go. And the moth was very grateful.

Now George and Jane went sliding on down the road...
until suddenly, it ended and they tumbled into soft snow.
Above them towered a column of ice, with blue
and green and pink fires burning all around it.

"The North Pole," breathed George.

"The Northern Lights," whispered Jane.

There was something else around the Pole, too –
something made of glassy ice, with an icy blue heart.

"What a strange shape," said George. "It's just like
a dragon. Look, there's the tail."

"Yes, and those are its wings," agreed Jane.

"You know, I think it really is a dragon,"
exclaimed George. "A frozen dragon!"

Just then, a troop of furry goblins appeared,
lugging bundles of firewood. "We'll feed the fires
until the dragon thaws," they chuckled. "When it comes
to life, it'll eat all the people and the world will be ours!"

One of the goblins spotted George and Jane. "Spies,"
it howled. "Quick, catch them!" Furry hands seized
George and Jane, and tied them to the frozen Pole.

"The dragon will eat you soon," giggled a goblin.
"If we don't freeze first," snapped George.

But before the cold could set in, a flock of geese flapped
overhead, led by the goose they had saved. Each dropped a
feather, until George and Jane were covered in a warm blanket.

A moment later, fluttering moths filled the air, led by the
moth they had freed. The goblins shrieked and ran away –
because moths eat fur, and the goblins were covered in fur.

The moths and geese chased after them.

"Wait, untie us..."
called George. But it was
too late. The animals were
gone. All the flapping and
fluttering had put out the
fires, so it was very dark and
cold – and getting colder every
second. George and Jane shivered,
even under their feather blanket.
"What shall we do?" said Jane,
trying to sound brave.
Suddenly, there was a loud
CRACK.
It was the dragon!
The goblins had been wrong – it was an ice
dragon and only came alive in extreme cold.
Now the fires were out, it was finally waking up.
As it clambered to its feet, it snapped the rope
tying George and Jane. "Quick," said George.
"I think it's heading for the road. Let's climb on."

So they crawled up the dragon's tail
and onto its back, and it didn't even notice.
George had been right. Soon, they were sliding back
over the icy road. The dragon went very fast, stopping only to
swallow two cross-looking men carrying a gun and a butterfly
net – because dragons do like to eat people occasionally.
But George and Jane were perfectly safe on his back.

Eventually they slid under a fence...
and through a hedge... and into their garden.
The bonfire was blazing brighter than ever. Before the
dragon knew what was happening, it had melted away,
leaving George and Jane sitting in a puddle.
"What an adventure," sighed Jane, stumbling to her feet.
Then she yawned. "But it's been a long night."
"Come on, let's go inside," said George.
"I think it's time for bed."

The Magic Nutcracker

It was Christmas Eve and it was snowing. Marie was sitting in the window with her brother, Fritz, waiting impatiently for her godfather to arrive.

Her godfather was a toymaker, but his toys weren't like anyone else's. They were beautifully carved and painted, and full of clever tricks. His tin soldiers could really march up and down, and his dolls could walk and talk. And now, he was coming with presents!

At last, they heard footsteps in the hall, and a tall man appeared, shaking the snow from his coat.

"Merry Christmas, Godfather!" cried Marie.

"Merry Christmas!" he replied, laughing and holding out two packages. For Fritz, there was a wonderful wooden castle, and for Marie, a wooden doll in a bright soldier's outfit.

"He's really a nutcracker," said her godfather, pulling out a handful of nuts to show her. Marie tried a hazelnut. The shell split neatly – crick-crack. But she nearly dropped her new toy in surprise.

"I... I think he winked at me," she whispered.

Fritz looked over. "Let me try," he said, choosing the biggest walnut. Crick-SNAP! The nut was too big and the nutcracker broke. Marie's face fell.

"I'll mend him tomorrow," promised her godfather.

"But now it's bedtime..."

Fritz ran off to brush his teeth, while Marie put their toys away in the toy chest. Suddenly, she heard a pitter-patter, like hundreds of tiny feet.

Then came a loud squeak: "Make way for the Mouse King!" A fat, proud-looking mouse in a golden crown appeared, followed by an army of mice.

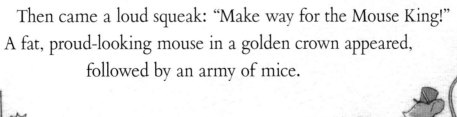

Marie backed nervously against the chest. To her astonishment, the nutcracker leaped to his feet beside her, perfectly whole again.

"Go back to your holes, mice!" he shouted. But the mice kept coming. The nutcracker frowned. "Toys to the rescue," he called bravely.

Amazed, Marie watched as all the dolls, teddies and other toys in the chest jumped up and began chasing the mice away.

But then the Mouse King raised his sword... Marie realized he was about to strike the nutcracker.

"Oh no," she gasped. She fumbled for her slipper and threw it, knocking his crown to the floor. The Mouse King fled, his army streaming after him.

The nutcracker turned to Marie. "You saved my life," he said, bowing. "Thank you. Will you come with me to a victory feast in the Land of Toys?"

Marie nodded and found herself shrinking. A set of steps appeared at the back of the toy chest. She followed the nutcracker up and out, into a meadow sparkling with sugar flowers. They walked on, through woods where toy monkeys climbed lollipop trees, to a river of fizzing lemonade.

A silver swan was waiting to carry them across, to a town built entirely of candy. There were gingerbread walls and chocolate roofs, and the streets were paved with sugared almonds.

Marie sniffed the air in delight.

Smiling dolls came out of the houses to cheer as they passed. The nutcracker led her to an elegant marzipan palace, where they feasted on sugar plums and toffee apples. Then some of the dolls began to dance, whirling and twirling over the marzipan floor.

Marie felt too full to join in. She yawned sleepily and closed her eyes – and when she opened them again, she was back in her own bed and it was morning.

"Was I dreaming?" she wondered. She leaped up and ran to the toy chest. "Ow!" She had stepped on a tiny golden crown.

The nutcracker was on his shelf, looking as good as new. And Marie was almost sure she saw him wink.

Fairy Gold

One moonlit evening, a tailor and a goldsmith were out walking when they heard music. They followed the sound and found a crowd of little folk, dancing merrily in a ring...

"Fairies!" cried the tailor in delight. They were a magical sight, with bright wings and beautiful faces.

The fairies asked the two men to join in. So they danced and danced, until they were out of breath, and then they dropped onto the ground to rest.

An old fairy with a white beard came to sit with them. He nodded kindly and offered each of them a lump of coal.

"How odd," muttered the goldsmith. But he never turned down free gifts, and the tailor didn't want to seem rude. So they thanked the old fairy politely and put the coal in their pockets.

Then, tired out from dancing, they curled up under their coats and fell asleep beneath the twinkling stars.

By daybreak, the fairies were gone. The tailor and the goldsmith woke groaning under the weight of something in their pockets. Mystified, they reached in – and each pulled out a heavy, gleaming lump of metal. The old fairy's coal had become solid gold!

"My luck is in," cried the tailor happily. "Now I can afford to marry my sweetheart." And he hurried off. "Aren't you coming?" he called back to the goldsmith.

The man shook his head. "Another lump and I'll be the richest man in town!" he replied. "I'm staying here."

At dusk, the fairies reappeared. The goldsmith joined in their dancing, just as before. And just as before, the old fairy handed him a lump of coal.

The goldsmith went to sleep dreaming of riches and, when he woke, felt eagerly in his pockets...

To his dismay, his fingers came out black and sooty.

"Noooo," he wailed. Frantically, he turned his pockets inside out. They contained nothing but coal.

So the greedy goldsmith lost his fortune – and shivered all winter. He refused to burn any coal, in case it turned into gold.

But the tailor and his sweetheart lived happily together for the rest of their days.

Seven Suns

Long ago, in China, everything was in a terrible state.
People went to bed at any old time, or didn't go to bed at all,
because as soon as the sun set, another sun – or two suns,
or three – would rise to take its place. So it was never,
ever dark, and it was always far too hot.

All in all, there were seven suns criss-crossing the sky.
When two suns shone, the crops wilted in the fields. If three
suns blazed, the windowsills grew hot enough to bake bread.
And when four suns burned, people had to sprinkle water
over the rooftops to stop them from catching fire.

People moaned and groaned,
but no one dared to do anything about it.
No one, that is, until Erlang...
Erlang was three times as strong as an ordinary
man, and nine times as brave. And he was determined
to sort out the suns. So he climbed to the top of the tallest
hill and waited.

As soon as a sun rolled overhead, Erlang leaped up and
snatched it out of the sky. "Gotcha!" It scorched his fingers,
but there was one less sun in the sky.

Then another sun drifted past. Erlang leaped again. But as
he grabbed it, the first sun slipped out of his grasp. "Drat!"

A third sun soared overhead. Erlang leaped –
and the second sun escaped...

And so it went on.

However hard Erlang tried, the suns kept getting away. After several hours, he was exhausted.

"It's no good," he muttered, sinking down onto the ground. "I need a better plan." A heap of pebbles caught his eye. "Hmm, that gives me an idea."

Erlang took a huge sack, stuffed it with pebbles, and waited for the next sun to come along. This time, when he'd caught it, he held it down and poured the pebbles over it, burying it so it couldn't escape. Then, he refilled the sack and started all over again.

Now, he caught sun after sun, and none escaped. As he buried each one, the sky grew darker and the air grew cooler. All in all, he buried six suns – but he was so tired, he lost count.

For a long time, Erlang saw no more suns. He waited with his pebbles. Suddenly, a ray peeked out from behind a cloud.

"There's one," he cried. "It's been hiding."

To his surprise, the sun spoke back. "Please don't hurt me, Erlang! I'm the only sun left in the sky."

Erlang rubbed his chin thoughtfully. "Well, we do need one sun," he agreed. "But you must promise to be good. Each morning, you must rise nicely and light up the sky. And each evening, you must go quietly to bed. People need your light, but they also have to sleep!"

"I promise!" said the sun, hurrying away quickly before Erlang could change his mind. True to its word, it went straight to bed.

As the sun sank below the horizon, the first night spread across the sky. It was beautifully cool and fresh and dark.

Erlang sighed happily and went home to bed.

Winter and Spring

Once, in Ancient Greece, there was no such thing as winter. Instead, Demeter, the Earth Goddess, made the sun shine brightly all year round. She made the crops grow and flowers bloom... and no one loved those flowers more than her daughter, Persephone.

One afternoon, Persephone was picking wild roses when she saw a dark chariot, pulled by four night-black horses. Pluto, God of the Underworld, was out riding.

Pluto lived in an underground realm of darkness and shadows. He was dazzled by the sight of Persephone, her hair shining like gold in the sunlight.

In that moment, he fell in love.

"She must be my queen," he decided.

"But how can I persuade her?"

Pluto frowned gloomily. Then, suddenly, he urged
his horses into a gallop. As they reached the startled girl,
he leaned down and lifted her into his chariot...

The horses raced on. At Pluto's command, a huge chasm
opened. The chariot plunged in and the ground closed with
a noise like thunder. Where Persephone had been, a few rose
petals drifted slowly down.

Eager to please, Pluto now showed Persephone the
treasures of his kingdom. He took her through fields of lilies to
enchanted rivers, and showered her with jewels dug from deep
under the ground... To his despair, Persephone just shrugged.
She was the daughter of a goddess, and not easily impressed.
"How dare you carry me off?" she snapped, for the
hundredth time. "My mother will be so worried."
"At least try to eat," begged Pluto.

He held out a plate piled
with rich red pomegranates.
"You've never tasted anything like these.
They're sweeter than any that grow above ground."
He smiled – a kind smile that lit up the darkness.
And Persephone couldn't help smiling back. Secretly,
she was starting to think Pluto was rather handsome...

Persephone was right about her mother. When she didn't
return, Demeter was frantic with worry.

She searched and searched, but her daughter was nowhere to be found. And then Demeter's sorrow chilled the land. Her sighs blew icy gusts and her tears fell as frozen rain, bringing the first winter.

Eventually, word reached Demeter that Pluto had taken Persephone to the Underworld.

"Pluto?" she screeched. "We'll see about that!" She went straight to Zeus, the King of the Gods.

"Pluto has stolen my daughter," she cried. "You must make him give her back. If not, I will create eternal winter."

Even mighty Zeus could not ignore such a threat. He sent a messenger to find Persephone at once.

Zeus sat on his throne with Demeter beside him, watching as the messenger returned with Persephone. To his surprise, Pluto had come too. Persephone trembled with nerves. Gently, Pluto took her hand.

Zeus looked searchingly at the young couple before speaking. "Demeter demands her daughter back... but first, Persephone, I must know if you ate anything in the Underworld? If you did, the law commands you stay."

Persephone bit her lip. "I didn't eat anything," she said. "Except..." She glanced at Demeter. "Except for four pomegranate seeds."

"So little!" cried Demeter. "Surely that doesn't count?"

Zeus looked at Persephone
and Pluto – who were still holding hands.
"I think it does," he said. "For each seed, Persephone will
spend one month of the year in the Underworld."
Pluto and Persephone smiled at each other, but Demeter
frowned. "Then for four months of the year, it will be
cold winter on earth," she snapped.
"So be it," decided Zeus.

Ever since, Demeter has marked her daughter's departure
by making the leaves fall and the flowers die. All the time
Persephone is with Pluto under the ground, winter freezes
the world. But when she returns, Demeter welcomes her
with sunshine and spring. And so the seasons change,
and Pluto and his young queen are content.
And Zeus watches from above and smiles.

Rip Van Winkle

Rip Van Winkle lived in the shadow of a majestic mountain range known as the Catskills. People told strange tales of the mountains, tales of ghosts and spirits, but Rip paid no attention. He loved the mountains and spent days wandering over their slopes – days when he should have been working in his fields.

This made Rip's wife cross. "Lazybones!" she would scold. "What will we eat if you don't plant the corn?"

Rip didn't have an answer. So he would just shrug and head back to the mountains. The more his wife scolded, the more time he spent away – and the more time he spent away, the more she scolded.

One sunny afternoon, Rip was drowsing in a warm
mountain meadow when he heard a voice.

"Rip," it called. "Rip Van Winkle!"

Rip turned, and saw a strange man clambering over
the rocks. He was short and squarely built, with a grizzled
beard and peculiar, old-fashioned clothes. He was struggling
to carry a huge wooden barrel and seemed to need help.
Rip hurried to lend a hand.

Rip grasped one end of the barrel and, without another
word, the man set off up the mountain. They carried the
barrel higher and higher, following a steep, stony path.
In the distance, Rip could hear a noise like thunder,
which grew louder and louder...

At last, they came to a gap in the rocks,
and the man stepped through, beckoning Rip
to follow. On the other side lay a valley –
and in the valley was a whole crowd of
people in old-fashioned clothes.

"Who are they?" Rip asked curiously.
But his companion didn't answer.

At first, none of the crowd noticed the new
arrivals. They were too busy rolling huge boulders at
a line of standing stones. The rocks rumbled and crashed,
and the noise echoed around the valley like thunder.
Slowly, Rip realized what was going on.

"They're bowling at ninepins!" he cried.

Rip's companion opened the barrel and a warm,
honeyed scent filled the air. Now, the players stopped and
turned to stare. Their lips moved, but no sound came out.
Rip gulped. He remembered the old ghost stories and his
knees began to tremble.

The man poured the barrel's contents into tin mugs,
and waved at Rip to pass them around. Nervously, Rip obeyed.
The crowd downed their drinks in silence and then returned
to their game.

Curious, Rip took a mug himself. The first mouthful
tasted so good, he had another... and another... and yawned.

The drink had made him sleepy. "Time for a nap,"
he decided, stretching out on the ground.

When Rip woke, it was morning.

"Oooh, I'm so stiff," he moaned. "I must have been out all night. Whatever will my wife say?"

He stumbled to his feet and looked around. There was no one in sight - only some mossy boulders and an old tin mug, falling apart with rust.

"That's strange," he muttered. "Time I got out of here, I think... where's that path?"

But where he thought the path should be, he found a foaming mountain stream. He picked his way down beside it, trying hard not to slip.

As he reached the farm, he grew more and more puzzled. Everything looked different somehow.

"Are you alright, Grandpa?" called a strange boy.

"Who are you calling Grandpa?" snapped Rip. But then he caught sight of his reflection in a window, and the words died on his lips. He had grown a beard a foot long.

"I wonder what was in that drink," he thought uneasily to himself. "Hair tonic?"

The front of his house was covered with rambling roses. "But we only planted those last week!" he exclaimed in bewilderment. "How long was I asleep?"

A pretty young woman was sitting on the porch. "Can I help you?" she asked politely.

"Is-isn't this Rip Van Winkle's house?" stuttered Rip.

"Rip Van Winkle was my father," she replied.
"But he disappeared in the mountains years ago..."

"Daughter?" said Rip. "Is that you?"

The young woman looked closer. "Father!" she yelled.
She jumped up and flung her arms around him. "We thought
you were gone forever... Mother!"

Her cries brought Mrs. Van Winkle running. When she
saw Rip, she stopped dead. "Oh, so you finally came back,"
she said - but she was smiling. Time had mellowed her temper.

"We missed you, you old rascal," she added. "Where
have you been?"

"You wouldn't believe me if I told you," laughed Rip.
"But I'm glad to be home. And this time, I promise I'll stay
and take care of you all. I've had enough of the mountains to
last me a lifetime!"

The Endless Day

It was nearly bedtime, but Will didn't want to
go to bed. He wanted to stay up with his new friend,
Robin Goodfellow.

Robin wasn't like Will's other friends. He had pointed
ears and funny clothes, and lived at the bottom of the garden.
He had been showing Will all sorts of magical things – how
to tell the time from a dandelion clock, and talk to the birds,
and find hidden treasure...

"I wish today could last forever," sighed Will, as the light
began to fade. "I don't want it ever to be night."

Robin chuckled. "That can be arranged," he said.

He reached up to the sky and pulled out a dark,
wispy thread. He pulled harder.

The thread thickened, until Robin seemed to be
holding a billowing black sheet. Then, he gave a sharp tug
and the whole thing came tumbling to the ground –
leaving the sky a dazzling blue.

"Now, go inside and look at the clock," said Robin.
Puzzled, Will went inside. His father was in the hall,
staring at the clock. The clock was ticking, but the
hands weren't moving.

"It must be broken," said his father, scratching his head.
"We'll just have to go to bed when it's dark."

But it wasn't getting dark.

"It was Robin," Will realized. "He's taken away
the night." He smiled and went back outside.

Robin and Will went on playing.

A little while later, Will found
himself stifling a yawn. He didn't want to admit it,
but he was tired. And still it didn't get dark.

Now, things didn't seem so much fun. After a while,
Will said goodbye and crept indoors. But when he tried to go
to bed, the sun shone through the curtains and kept him awake.

Outside, he could hear an owl hooting crossly.

"Too much light, too-whoo..." it called.

"Who-oo took away the dark?"

Will opened the window and leaned out.

"Please, Mr. Owl," he called. "I told Robin I wanted
the day to last forever, and he took the dark out of the sky."

"That was foo-oo-oolish," hooted the owl. "You'd better ask
him to put it back!"

So Will went to look for Robin. He found him under a tree,
munching on an apple.

"Back already? What shall we do next?" asked Robin.

"Nothing, thank you," said Will. "Please, Robin, will you
put the dark back? It's too bright to sleep."

"You should have thought of that," snapped Robin.
"I go to all that trouble and now you want me to put it back!"

Will tried to argue, but he didn't know how.
He was so tired, he could barely think straight.
Then – he couldn't help himself – he just yawned.

Yawning, as everyone knows, is catching.
Moments later, Robin yawned too.
"Now you're making me sleepy,"
he grumbled. "I think I need forty winks.
Hmm, perhaps you're right."
He pulled out what looked like a dark pocket
handkerchief and gave it a shake...
At last, darkness spread across the land, covering
everything like a soft, warm blanket. In the trees,
the owl hooted happily. Will's eyelids drooped.
"Time for bed," said Robin gently.
"Good night!"

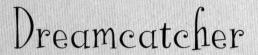

Dreamcatcher

Darkness was falling and little Okemos* was tucked up in bed
– but he was still wide awake. He was too scared to go to sleep,
in case there were nightmares waiting for him...

"You must sleep sometime," came a tiny voice.

Okemos looked up and saw a spider.

"I can help you," promised the spider. "Nothing gets past
my webs! I will weave a web to catch bad dreams, so you
can sleep in peace."

As Okemos watched, the spider set to work. She went
around and around, like the sun going around the earth.

And then she went back and forth, and in and out...

until there was a neatly spun web, glimmering
and shimmering in the firelight.

"That will stop any nightmares," she promised.

"What about that hole?" cried Okemos, pointing to a tiny
gap in the middle.

"That's for good dreams to get through," replied the spider.
"But I haven't finished yet..."

*Say Oh-kee-muss

Now the spider scuttled away
and came back with some feathers –
two soft, speckled owl feathers, and a
big, strong eagle feather.

She hung the eagle feather from the
bottom of the web. "That is to make you
brave, like an eagle," she told Okemos.

And on either side, she put an owl
feather. "And wise, like an owl," she added.

The feathers dangled from the web,
twirling and whirling in every breath
of air. Okemos smiled as he watched them.
Then he yawned. And finally, he fell asleep.

All night long, he dreamed sweet
dreams. Just as the spider promised, not a
single nightmare got through. Instead, the
bad dreams stuck to the web – until the sun
rose and touched them with light, and they
fizzled away into nothing.

And when Okemos woke, the first thing
he saw was the web sparkling in the sunshine
and the feathers dancing in the wind.

Hercules and the Golden Apples

Hercules was the biggest, boldest, bravest warrior in all of Ancient Greece. He had promised to serve the King of Tiryns, but his huge strength made the king nervous. So the king kept sending Hercules on impossible tasks, to try to get rid of him.

Hercules had fought fearsome lions, terrible monsters and mighty warriors... and so far, he had always won.

Now the king was trying to think of a fresh challenge. "I know," he exclaimed. "Bring me some golden apples from the tree of the gods!"

Even Hercules looked taken aback. "No human has ever seen that tree," he cried. "How am I supposed to find it?"

"That's part of the task," insisted the king. "Off you go – and don't come back without my apples."

Hercules set off at once. He searched and searched, across Asia, Africa and Arabia...

but there were no golden apples anywhere.

At last, a water nymph took pity on him.

"Only a god can tell you where to find the tree," she said.

"Look there on the shore – it's the sea god, Nereus, sleeping. Catch him before he wakes and he'll have to help you."

Grinning, Hercules tiptoed up to the god and seized him with a grip like iron. "I'm not letting go until you tell me how to find the golden apples!" he yelled.

Nereus struggled, but Hercules was too strong. Then the sea god summoned his magic. Suddenly, Hercules found himself holding a flapping fish...

a slippery sea snake...

a slimy squid...

but he held on tight.

Finally, an angry octopus turned back
into Nereus, looking tired and grumpy.
"All right, you win," he growled. "The tree
grows on an island at the edge of the Western
Ocean. But you won't be able to pick the apples
yourself – the tree is guarded by a dragon that
never sleeps, and the daughters of the giant, Atlas.
You'll have to persuade Atlas to help you."

So Hercules journeyed to the great mountain of Atlas.
The giant crouched on top of the highest peak, supporting
the weight of the sky on his shoulders.
"Will you help?" asked Hercules, after explaining his quest.
"I'd like to," answered Atlas. "But even I can't get past that
dragon. It's got a hundred heads watching in all directions at once."
"A hundred heads?" snorted Hercules.
"Well, I'm used to monsters! Where is it?"

Atlas pointed to a tiny island on the horizon. Hercules narrowed his eyes. He could just make out a fearsome, snake-like creature coiled around a tree. "Let's see what it makes of this," he muttered, pulling out his bow.

Twang! From the bow, a single arrow soared through the sky – and sank deep into the dragon's heart. The monster sighed and slumped to the ground, stone dead.

Hercules turned back to Atlas. "Now will you help?"

"I'd like to," answered Atlas again. "But if I leave here, the sky will come crashing down... unless you're strong enough to take my place while I get the apples?"

Hercules flexed his muscles. "I can do that," he said, reaching upward.

"Ah, that feels good," sighed Atlas, as the weight lifted. He stretched gratefully, then strode off over the ocean.

Strong as he was, Hercules felt as if the weight of the sky
would crush him. Every muscle straining, he watched anxiously
as Atlas reached the island. In the middle stood a tree glinting
with golden fruit, the dragon curled lifelessly around its trunk.
Three sisters, each as beautiful as the evening star,
came running to greet their father.

72

"I've come for some apples," Atlas told them.

Each sister ran up to the magical tree and plucked one of the heavy golden fruit. Then, Atlas came striding home...

"At last," croaked Hercules, sweating under his burden. "Here, have the sky back."

Atlas looked crafty. "It's too heavy," he replied. "You keep it! I'll take these apples to the king myself. If he wants them so much, I'm sure he'll reward me."

Hercules thought quickly. "All right," he said. "I'm sure you deserve some time off. But I'm very uncomfortable like this. Could you hold the sky for just a moment, while I get into a better position?"

Atlas agreed. But as soon as he took the sky again, Hercules grabbed the apples and ran...

"Come back!" roared Atlas. "You tricked me."

"You tricked me first," Hercules laughed. "I only outwitted you at your own game."

Atlas was furious, but there was nothing he could do.

He had to go on holding up the sky.

As for Hercules, he brought back the apples back to the king in triumph. The people cheered, and the gods smiled on his success. And later, so his daring deeds would always be remembered, the gods placed him among the stars along with the dragon he defeated - where they still shine to this day.

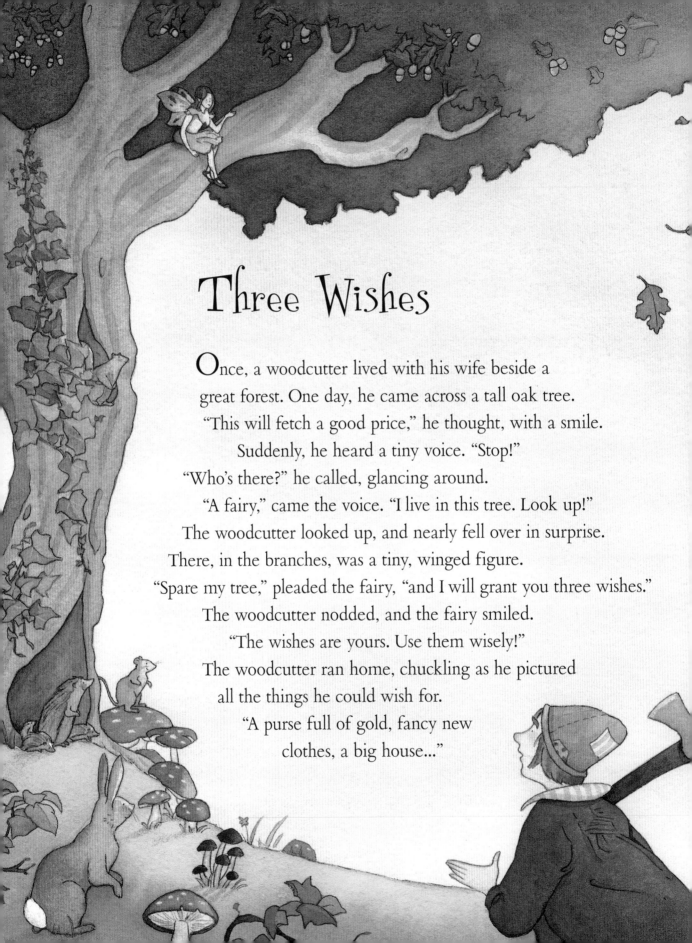

Three Wishes

Once, a woodcutter lived with his wife beside a
great forest. One day, he came across a tall oak tree.
"This will fetch a good price," he thought, with a smile.
Suddenly, he heard a tiny voice. "Stop!"
"Who's there?" he called, glancing around.
"A fairy," came the voice. "I live in this tree. Look up!"
The woodcutter looked up, and nearly fell over in surprise.
There, in the branches, was a tiny, winged figure.
"Spare my tree," pleaded the fairy, "and I will grant you three wishes."
The woodcutter nodded, and the fairy smiled.
"The wishes are yours. Use them wisely!"
The woodcutter ran home, chuckling as he pictured
all the things he could wish for.
"A purse full of gold, fancy new
clothes, a big house..."

"What should I ask for first?"

"You're early," said his wife when she saw him. "Dinner won't be ready for ages."

"Oh no, I'm starving," moaned the woodcutter. "I wish I had a nice, fat sausage." And – lo and behold – a fat, glistening sausage instantly appeared on the table.

His wife stared. "How did you do that?" she asked.

"Three wishes," said the woodcutter proudly. And he explained about the fairy in the tree.

"Idiot!" snapped his wife. "You could have wished for anything, and you wished for a sausage! I wish your stupid sausage was on the end of your nose, that's what I wish. Oh no! I didn't mean it," she gasped – but too late. The sausage now dangled greasily from her husband's nose.

"Sorry," she said, trying not to laugh. She grabbed the sausage and gave it a sharp tug.

"Ow!" yelled the woodcutter.

"It won't budge," she admitted. "But we've still got a wish left... what will it be? We can be rich, but you'd have to spend the rest of your life with a sausage-nose!"

"What good would that be?" muttered the woodcutter glumly. "I'd never be able to show my face again."

His wife nodded. "Then I wish the sausage was back on the table," she said – and it was. "So much for our three wishes," she sighed. "But at least we'll have sausage for dinner!"

Twelve Months

Mariya and Zina were sisters, but they couldn't have been more different. All winter long, Zina grumbled and groaned. "I can't stand the bad weather," she moaned. "I long for fresh violets... Mariya, see if you can find some!"

So kind-hearted Mariya picked up her shawl and went out into the cold. The wind howled and frost nipped her fingers, but she kept looking.

After a while, she came to a hilltop where some people were warming themselves at a fire. Mariya peered through the smoke. There were twelve of them, all men. The flames crackled invitingly in the icy air.

"Hello," she said politely. "Please may I warm myself at your fire?"

The men made room for her, and soon they were all chatting happily.

"Why are you out in this weather?" asked one, who said his name was March.

"My sister sent me out for violets," replied Mariya.

March smiled. "I can help." He tapped the ground and,
at once, a patch of little purple flowers sprang up.

"Thank you!" cried Mariya, astonished, and she gathered
a bunch to take home.

Flowers weren't enough for Zina. "I'm hungry,"
she complained. "Can't you get some strawberries?"

Once more, Mariya picked up her shawl...

The men were still around the fire – and surprised
to see her back so soon.

"My sister sent me for strawberries," she explained.

"Then you need me," said a man with sunny golden hair.
"I'm June." He waved his hand and a clump of plants appeared,
bursting with berries. Mariya thanked him and and went
home with a juicy handful.

Zina scowled at the strawberries. "I'd rather have an apple!"
she sniffed. So Mariya went out again...

"Hello again," said the men, laughing.

"What is it now?"

"Please, my sister would like an apple."

A man with nut-brown eyes tapped a tree – which was
suddenly covered in rustling leaves and ripe apples.
"A gift from September," he said, with a wink.
Mariya thanked him and picked a few to take home.

"Is that all?" cried Zina greedily, when Mariya showed her.
"You should have brought a sackful!" She snatched Mariya's
shawl and rushed off to look for more.
When she got to the fire, she pushed her way into the
warmth. "Where are my apples?" she snapped.
The men frowned. Then, snowy-haired January spoke.
"I'll give you the gift you deserve," he said icily. He clapped
his hands and a freezing blizzard blew up.
Zina had to run home empty-handed.
But Mariya often visited the fire on the hilltop,
and always enjoyed the freshest flowers and fruit, for all
twelve months were now her faithful friends.

The Magic Pear Tree

It was market day and the streets were bustling with crowds buying fruit and vegetables. On one corner stood a wooden barrow piled high with plump, golden pears. They smelled as sweet as honey – although the farmer selling them looked as sour as a lemon.

A monk in ragged old robes stopped by the barrow and smiled. "Please, may I have a pear?" he asked.

"Can you pay for it?" snapped the farmer. "If not, go away and stop bothering me."

"I have no money," said the monk. "But you have so many pears, surely you can spare one?"

"Go on, give him one," said a man selling tea nearby. The farmer ignored him. The tea-seller looked at the monk's thin features. Then he pulled out a coin and paid for a pear.

The monk ate hungrily, bite after juicy bite, until there was nothing left but a handful of seeds. "Thank you," he said to the tea-seller. "That was very kind. Now, I would like to give you one of MY pears."

"What pears?" cried the tea-seller in surprise.

"If you have your own pears, why are you eating mine?" grumbled the farmer.

"I just needed a few seeds," said the monk. He bent down, scraped a little hole and scattered the seeds in it. "Now, for some water," he added.

The tea-seller passed him a kettle.

"Stand back," warned the monk.

As soon as water touched the seeds, a green shoot sprang up. In moments, it thickened into a trunk, sprouting branches, twigs and leaves. Then flower buds appeared, opened and, in the blink of an eye, ripened into plump, golden pears.

The monk picked the sweet-smelling fruit and passed them around. Everyone in the market got one – even the grumpy farmer. When all the pears were gone, the monk borrowed a hatchet, chopped down the tree and strolled away.

Scratching his head, the farmer finally turned back to his barrow – only to find it empty. Suddenly, he realized... "Those pears weren't magic – they were mine!" he yelled. "That monk's a thief!"
He grabbed his barrow and tried to run after the monk, but the handle fell apart in his hands. It had been chopped through with a hatchet. Everyone around him burst out laughing. "Maybe next time you'll be quicker to share your good fortune with others," chuckled the tea-seller.

Stone Soup

As dusk fell, an old soldier trudged into the village,
on his way home from the wars. His boots were worn
and his coat was torn, but he whistled merrily, as if he didn't
have a care in the world.

"I've been walking for miles," he said. "Can you give me
a meal and a bed for the night?"

The villagers exchanged glances. Times were hard and they
didn't want to share their food with a stranger.

"You can sleep in my barn," offered one. "But...
I'm afraid we've nothing to eat."

"Really?" exclaimed the soldier, reaching into his pocket. "Nothing at all? Then it's lucky for you I came along! I'll feed all of us tonight – with this." And he opened his hand to reveal a small, round stone.

"A stone?" laughed the villagers. "You can't eat that!"

"Ah, but this is no ordinary stone," explained the soldier. "If you put it in water, it brews the most delicious soup. I can show you how, if you like. I'll just need a pot of water and some firewood."

Well, that was not much to ask, so the villagers agreed. Soon, a huge pot was bubbling away merrily.

The villagers watched as the soldier added the stone, stirred the pot, and tasted it.

"Well?" they asked eagerly.

"Mmm... not bad," said the soldier. "Maybe a little thin. Good stone soup really needs a bit of potato. But never mind! We'll make do with what we've got."

"Um... I have a few potatoes at home," said one man.

"Splendid!" cried the soldier. "I promise you'll never taste anything as good as stone soup with potato."

The man got his potatoes and the soldier stirred them in. Then he tasted the soup again.

"Much better!" he declared. "Although it'd be even nicer with an onion or two. Still, beggars can't be choosers."

"I have some onions," said a woman shyly.

"Great!" said the soldier. "We'll have a real feast now."

The woman brought the onions and the soldier stirred them in. A rich, oniony smell wafted out of the pot.

The soldier tried the soup again.

"Very tasty," he said. "I'm just sorry there's no ham. The best stone soup always has a bit of ham."

"We have some ham," said a girl – and ran to get it.

By now, everyone was starving. The soldier stirred in the ham and tasted the soup again. "Mmm, that's good," he sighed. "A few extra vegetables would make it absolutely perfect... but you can't have everything!"

The remaining villagers looked at each other sheepishly. Then, one by one, they crept away and came back with whatever they could: a bunch of carrots, a cabbage or a handful of peas...

The soldier stirred everything in, until the pot brimmed with thick, hearty soup. Everyone watched anxiously as he tried another spoonful.

"Delicious!" he declared. "Absolutely delicious. This is the best stone soup ever."

And it was.

"Who'd have thought a stone would make such good soup?" cried the villagers, between slurps. "We must make this again."

The old soldier grinned. "You can keep the stone," he said. "Just remember the recipe. A little from everyone, and you won't go wrong."

The Man in the Moon

The Sultan of Turkey owned many rare and wonderful things, but most wonderful of all were his giant silver bees. Each day, the sultan's bee-keeper herded the bees out to pasture, and each night he collected their precious golden honey.

But one day, a gust of wind caught one of the bees and whirled it away. It blew up through the clouds, higher and higher, until it blew into the moon.

"Oh no," cried the bee-keeper, squinting after it. "The sultan will be furious! I must get it back... But how?" He looked around and saw some beans. "I wonder..." He took one, planted it in a little hole and sprinkled it with water.

Very soon, a vine shot up. It snaked through the clouds, higher and higher, until it twined around the moon. The bee-keeper smiled and began to climb, up through the clouds, higher and higher...

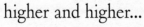

At last, he found himself in a
strange moonscape, full of rocks and craters,
all glowing with a silvery light.
"Why, everything here looks silver," he exclaimed.
"I hope I can find my bee."
He searched crater after crater, until eventually he heard a
faint buzzing. It was the bee, and it was very glad to see him.
The bee-keeper carried it back to the vine. "What an adventure,"
he sighed. "I can't wait to tell everyone. But will they believe me?
I should do something to show I was here."
He thought for a moment, then drew a picture of his face in the
dust. "Won't they be surprised to see a man in the moon," he
chuckled, as he grasped the vine and began the long climb down...

Back at home, the bee-keeper went on happily herding bees.
He took great care to avoid the wind, so he never had to climb
to the moon again. But if you look up, on some bright night,
you may still make out his picture of a man in the moon.

The Sun
and the Wind

It was a beautiful spring day, and the Sun was smiling brightly – but everyone was shivering, because a cold Wind was howling through the sky.

"Look at me!" roared the Wind, setting the treetops tossing. "I'm so strong – even stronger than you, Sun."

"Really?" replied the Sun. "I'm not so sure...

I know! Let's have a contest to decide."

He looked down and spotted a man walking along in a thick winter coat. "You see that man? Let's see which of us can remove his coat."

"All right," said
the Wind confidently.
"Watch this." He huffed and he
puffed, and he blew the man's hat right off his head.
"Now for his coat," cried the Wind, puffing harder still...
The man was almost blown off his feet - but he just clutched
his coat tightly around himself and kept on walking.

"That's no way to go about it," said the Sun, laughing.
"Watch this." And he beamed down upon the man...
The man smiled as golden sunshine warmed the air.
All around him, flowers opened and birds began to sing.
One by one, he undid his coat buttons, and still the Sun shone
down. Now it was so warm, the man began to feel sleepy.
Yawning, he took off his coat and spread it on the grass -
then lay down and fell asleep, dreaming of the summer to come.
"You see," whispered the Sun to the Wind.
"A little gentleness goes a long way."

The Magic Carpet

Princess Nura didn't know what to do. Three different princes wanted to marry her, and she didn't know who to choose.

"Hasan is so handsome," she sighed. "But Ahmed is so clever. And Ali always makes me laugh."

"Why don't you set us a challenge?" suggested Ahmed.

"All right," agreed the princess. "I'll marry whoever brings me the rarest treasure!"

So the princes set off. They searched far and wide, in bustling bazaars and ancient antique shops. Nothing seemed special enough – until one day, Ali met a blue-eyed woman who handed him an ivory telescope. "What does it do?" he asked.

"It shows whatever you want to see," replied the woman. Ali took a peek, and saw Nura – looking more beautiful than ever. "I'll buy it!" he exclaimed.

A little later, Ahmed met a blue-eyed woman who offered him a sweet-smelling apple. It had a wonderful scent, but Ahmed wasn't sure. "It's just an apple," he sighed.

"Yes, but its smell cures any illness," the woman told him. Ahmed bought it at once.

90

Hasan had still found nothing. He was walking through a busy market when he noticed a blue-eyed woman with a carpet for sale. The carpet was old and worn – but when the woman smiled at him, his spine tingled, and he offered to buy it anyway.

"You are wise," she told him, as he gave her his money. "This is a magic carpet. It will carry you wherever you wish, over seas or mountains. Try it!"

Hasan stepped onto the carpet. "Up," he commanded. The carpet quivered and rose... Hasan gasped as the market stalls shrank to the size of toys. "This is amazing!"

Suddenly, he spotted Ali and Ahmed. They were hurrying along, looking worried.

"What's the matter?" he called, swooping down.

Ali waved an ivory telescope. "I saw Nura," he cried.

"She's been taken sick!"

"But I can cure her with this apple," added Ahmed.
"If we can only get there in time."

"No problem," answered Hasan. "Climb aboard!"

The carpet sped through the air, towards the gleaming domes of the palace. Minutes later, they landed beside Nura. She was terribly pale. But as soon as she smelled the apple, pink returned to her cheeks.

Nura was very impressed with all three treasures. "But they're equally wonderful," she said. "So I still can't decide. We need a new challenge. I know! Who can shoot furthest?"

The princes fetched their bows.

Ahmed was first. His arrow went far, but Ali's went further. Then it was Hasan's turn. His arrow soared into the sky – and vanished.

"That's a forfeit," said Ali. "I win!" He turned to the princess and bowed. "Will you be mine?"

"Yes," replied Nura, laughing happily.

Ahmed sighed and turned away – only to notice another girl.

She gave him a shy smile and his heart leaped. "She's even lovelier than Nura," he thought. "Who can she be?"

"Let me introduce you to my sister," said Nura.

Ahmed laughed. "It seems things have worked out for the best," he decided.

Now Hasan was all alone. "I want to find out where my arrow went." He unrolled the carpet. "Take me to it!"

Soon, he was flying above a golden desert.

Then he glimpsed water. "An oasis!"

The carpet landed by the water's edge. Tall palm trees and sweet-smelling flowers grew all around. The blue-eyed woman was standing there, holding the arrow.

"Are you a fairy?" asked Hasan.

"Yes," she said. "Forgive me for magicking away your arrow, but I couldn't let you win. The princess really loved Ali."

"I'm glad," admitted Hasan. "Especially to see you again." He blushed and added, "I think I'd like to marry you."

The fairy smiled. "Nothing would make me gladder," she told him. "Now we can all live happily ever after – and that's the best magic of all."

About the Stories

The Bedtime Fairy was written specially for this book, but the other stories are based on traditional tales from around the world. Here, you can find out a little about their background.

Fairy Moon ◦ *Fairy Gold* ◦ *Elves and the Shoemaker*
These are old German fairy tales, first written down by brothers Jacob and Wilhelm Grimm in the early 1800s.

Sandman
A tale by Hans Christian Andersen, a poor Danish boy who made his fortune by writing stories.

Starlight Wishes ◦ *Tom Thumb* ◦ *Three Wishes*
These are English Fairy tales, collected by Joseph Jacobs.

Endless Day
This was inspired by English folklore about a mischievous fairy, Robin Goodfellow (also known as Puck).

Sun and the Wind ◦ *Miller's boy and the Mermaid*
These are fables by Aesop, a former slave who lived over 2,500 years ago in Ancient Greece.

Magic Nutcracker
Best-known as a ballet, this version is based on the story by 19th-century French writer, Alexandre Dumas.

Winter and Spring ◦ *Hercules*
   These are retellings of myths from Ancient Greece.

Fisherman and the Genie ◦ *Magic Carpet*
   These are old stories from a collection known as *The Arabian Nights*.

Stone Soup
   A tale from Eastern Europe, also known as *Nail Soup*.

Rip Van Winkle
   A short story by American writer, Washington Irving.

Man in the Moon
   This is adapted from a book by Rudolf Raspe, a German scientist and inventor of tall tales, who lived in the 1700s.

Clever Kallie
   This is an old Greek fairy tale.

Twelve Months
   This is a traditional Russian fairy tale.

Ice Dragon
   This is based on a story by English children's writer, E. Nesbit.

Seven Suns ◦ *Magic Pear Tree*
   These are folk tales from China.

Dreamcatcher
   This was inspired by native American folklore.

Digital manipulation by Nick Wakeford
US Editor: Carrie Armstrong

First published in 2008 by Usborne Publishing Ltd,
83-85 Saffron Hill, London, EC1N 8RT, England.
www.usborne.com